# MYTHED CONNECTIONS:

## A SHORT STORY COLLECTION OF CLASSICAL MYTH IN THE MODERN WORLD

BY

# MICHAEL G. MUNZ

Red Muse Press

Seattle WA 2017

Proofread by Vanya Drumchiiska

*This is a work of fiction. Names, characters, places, brands, media,
and incidents are either the product of the author's imagination or
are used fictitiously. Any resemblance to similarly named places or
to persons living or deceased is unintentional.*

Print ISBN 978-0-9977622-3-5

*For the Muse . . . and the god of paperback books.*

# TABLE OF CONTENTS

*"Everything comes in threes."*

*"Except when it doesn't."*

*—First and Second Laws of Cosmological Organization*

# FOREWORD

Welcome to *Mythed Connections*! The three stories in this collection are the result of my own amusement with the idea of what might happen if characters from Greek mythology were running around in our modern world. It was a thought that first inspired me in 2002 when "Playing with Hubris" was first written (though it wasn't published until a couple of years later when a little mag called *Nexgen Pulp* picked it up). The concept eventually led me to write an entire novel on the subject entitled *Zeus is Dead: A Monstrously Inconvenient Adventure*, which has won numerous honors since its original publication in July 2014.

In a sense, these three stories can be considered prequels to that forthcoming novel, as I drew on aspects from each of them in writing it. Marcus from "The Atheist and the Ferryman" has a cameo. Hermes once again puts to good use his English accent and sense of mischief seen in "Snipe Hunt."

But it's "Playing with Hubris" that lends the most: Apollo, always my favorite of the Greek pantheon, is a main character in *Zeus is Dead*. The café setting from the story has more than a few echoes in one of the early chapters in the novel. And, as for Thalia, well, just you try to keep a muse out of a book and see how well you do.

As a special bonus in this print edition of *Mythed Connections*, an excerpt from *Zeus Is Dead* is included somewhere in the back, possibly even with the words in the proper order. For those yet to read that novel, may it whet your appetite. For those who have already read it, you can tear out those pages and throw them at someone who hasn't.

Enjoy! And never mock old men in shacks on the shore of the Acheron.

Or do.

Your choice, really.

—Michael G. Munz

# THE ATHEIST AND THE FERRYMAN

That cat was going to be the death of him, and Marcus was beginning to suspect it was intentional.

"Faaaaagles!"

His voice echoed around the stalactites that dripped lime from the cave ceiling. When no answer came, he continued forward with three questions in his mind: Just where did that cat think it was going? What was making that light ahead? And exactly how long had there been a cave in his basement without him knowing about it?

A rocky step crumbled beneath his foot. He caught himself, tested the surface beside it, and then called out again. "Faaaagles!"

Again, there was no response. What did he expect to hear, anyway?

"Fagles," he muttered to himself. "Who the hell names a cat Fagles?" He moved on, flashlight clutched, feet cautious.

His girlfriend, he reminded himself, named a cat Fagles. At least she didn't call it Fluffy or Mister Pookums. Marcus considered himself open-minded, but he doubted he could date someone who would name a cat Fluffy. He barely even liked cats, but when you're seeing a woman like Miranda, you put up with the cat.

It naturally followed that if she asked you to take care of it for the weekend and it dashes into your basement when you try to give it its ear medicine, falls down a hole, and runs away, you go after it. Modern men made sacrifices for their women. That's the way it was, and now Marcus was trudging through a cave chasing after a woman's cat.

There was a dirty joke in there somewhere, he realized.

Yet where was that light coming from? There had to be a shaft ahead that let in some sunlight from the surface. That corner of his basement had always been a little too chilly. "Like a ghost walking through you," his superstitious grandma would've said. Now Marcus knew why. He'd have to block it up when he got back. That he'd never seen it before irked him to no end.

He reached the bottom of the natural staircase and yelled again. "Fagles! Come on, you damned cat, get—"

Marcus rounded a corner and halted.

"What the hell?"

It was easily the largest underground cavern he'd ever seen. (Not that he'd seen many, but it seemed impossible that anything larger could exist.) Hell, it seemed impossible that *this* one could, yet there it was. The source of the glow was still indiscernible but seemed to emanate from a point beyond the horizon marked by a range of cliffs. There appeared to be buildings there, though the distance and scarcity of the light made it impossible to tell their detail or purpose. Between the cliffs and the slope on which he stood ran a wide, meandering river that stretched into darkness on either side. A path, needlessly twisted, ran down to a small shack, a boat, and a dock along the shore.

But, he realized, no cat. How fast could an animal that size run?

He shut off his flashlight and trotted down the path toward the shore. Geez, anyone living down here stood a good chance of being barking mad. If they did see a cat, they'd probably eat it. How would he explain that to Miranda?

Talk to the madman, or break his girlfriend's heart? He'd rather face the madman. Marcus moved to knock at the door.

It opened before he touched it. A tall, gaunt man stepped out, robed in black and dread. Without a single acknowledging glance, he walked past Marcus toward the boat.

"Um, hello," Marcus started. The man stopped to pick up a long, dangerous looking staff. "Ah, there's no need for that. I'm just looking for a cat."

The man continued his steady stride toward the boat, climbed in, and turned to face him. The boat did not rock an inch.

"I don't mean to bother you," Marcus continued, "but if you've seen it, you'd really help me out."

The man stretched out an arm to point across the water in utter silence. Marcus waited for him to elaborate. All he got was an empty, chilling stare.

"The cat went across the water?" Marcus tried. "Is that what you're trying to tell me?" This was absurd. Cats didn't swim.

He took a few steps toward the man. "Can't you speak at all?" Frustration overpowered caution, and soon Marcus was directly next to him, as close as he could be without climbing into the boat.

The robed man lowered his arm and turned to regard Marcus for the first time, revealing a weathered face wrapped in dreadfully pale skin. His eyes searched Marcus's face with irises that were nearly clear. He stood perfectly still.

Hypnotically still.

In fact, the old man hardly seemed to breathe at all.

"Do you know," the man said at last, "how long it has been since I have seen a single living person?" It was a statement more than a question, and devoid of any relief that would imply the man wished a rescue.

It still gave Marcus pause. "How long have you been down here?"

The old man grinned. Slowly. "Oh," he answered, "long time." He stepped out of the boat with a grunt. "You . . . shouldn't be here, however. I would have told you sooner, but conversing with most people I see here is usually a waste of breath."

"I thought I was the first person you'd seen in a long time?"

The man shuffled away toward the shack. "First *living* person," he corrected. "The dead aren't usually worth talking to when I see them. Too many questions, always the same: 'Where am I?' 'What happened?' Gets tiresome. I'm not a tour guide; I'm a ferryman. And you," he suddenly turned, "shouldn't be here."

Marcus blinked. "Hey, I've got just as much right to be here as you do. This cave's made my house drafty for who knows how long. You see dead people, huh? Right. I don't know how long you've been down here or what you think you're doing, but I'm plugging up that hole as soon as I get back."

"There are other paths," the old man said. "Plug it. It matters not. Or perhaps it would make the dead angry. Who can say?"

"Look, I don't have time to listen to your delusions. Just tell me where my girlfriend's cat went and spare me the quasi-spiritual crap."

The old man stopped at the door to his shack. "You do not," he said, "belong here." With that, he shut the door.

"Hey!" Marcus rapped on the door. "You never

answered me about the cat!" He waited, but the man gave no response. "Senile old nut job," Marcus grumbled.

Unsure of what to do, he walked back up the embankment and sat himself down on a boulder. Seeing dead people. Right. It was ridiculous. When you're dead, you're dead. No spirit, no afterlife, no Creator. Spirituality was nothing more than a con game, and the crazy old man probably really believed it. Hell, he lived down here. He probably *did* eat the cat. At the very least, it was likely in his shack with him. There was nowhere else in sight for it to go.

"Fagles!" he called out again. "Fa—"

He stopped in mid-yell as a group of people stepped out of the cavern entrance and made their way down the path to the shore. Each wore an expression of confusion in direct opposition to the purpose of their stride.

Suddenly uneasy, Marcus tried to remain unseen as he watched them make their way down to the dock. As before, the old man left his shack and stepped wordlessly to the boat. They followed, boarding after him. There were six, and four of them handed the ferryman something that glinted in the dim, orange light. Was that gold? What kind of con was this guy running? Had all of those people come through his basement?

Marcus waited until the boat had left the shore and then crept down to the shack. Inside it was dark and windowless but for a hole in the roof above a small fire pit. A candle burned by the door, and Marcus took it as he entered. It shone on little else but a poor straw mattress, a chest, and what appeared to be a trap door in the far corner. No clothes. No closet. No odds and ends. What did the man do down here?

There was no sign of Fagles.

Remembering the glint he'd seen, Marcus tried the chest. Was this where he kept all the spoils from whatever con he was running? Though it was locked, the weight and the sound it made when Marcus tried to move it made it quite likely. Marcus gritted his teeth as he recalled the evangelist hucksters who'd bilked his grandma out of her savings. He'd find Fagles, yes, but he'd find out what else was happening here as well.

Then the light dimmed suddenly and Marcus looked behind him. The door was closed. Strange, he'd thought he'd left it open, and he didn't hear it shut. He crept back to it before he realized he had done so and opened it again. The door gave a labored creak. There was no sign of the old man or the boat. He had time.

He slipped back inside with the intent of checking the trap door. If he found half-eaten cat remains, he was going to be very disturbed, but he more than half expected—

Something moved.

The sound came from the trap door—or near it, at least. It sounded again, a scratching that slid up the wall, back down, and then ceased.

"Fagles?" he called. Damn, now he'd have to check.

The trap door was heavier than it looked, but unlocked. Lifting it a crack yielded only the sound of lapping water below. He carefully pushed it up further until it rested against the wall and then leaned on it with one arm while holding the candle in the other. There was only the river below. His reflection stared up from the water. Candlelight flickered back at him.

Then the flame's reflection vanished, and the face looking up at him was not his own.

Marcus jumped, dropped the candle and toppled forward, off-balance, into the water.

\* \* \*

He woke to find his clothes soaked, his muscles aching, and his back flat on the worn rocks of the shore. With a groan at the stiffness wrapping his body, Marcus forced himself up to sitting and realized he was downstream of the shack. The old man's boat was back at the dock.

How long had he been out? He couldn't even recall why he'd blacked out in the first place. There'd been a face. Yes, the face had startled him, and he'd fallen. He must've hit his head on the way down. Such an idiot. Smoke and mirrors, that's all it was. All part of the scam.

A minute later, he was pounding on the door of the shack. "Hey in there! I want some answers!"

"You were told. You do not belong here," came a whisper behind him.

Marcus turned with a start. The ferryman moved quietly if he—

He stopped in mid-thought. No one was there.

The door creaked behind him. Marcus turned again to find the ferryman in the doorway.

"Stop that," Marcus told him.

"Stop . . . what?"

"Stop, ya know, jumping around. Trying to mess with my head."

"Jumping around?" the old man asked. He grinned languidly, eyes glazed. "I was in my home." The grin darkened, tightening into a frown. "*You* were in my home."

Marcus stepped back. "Your home? You're using a path from *my* basement to get people here for this scam! I've got just as much right to be here as you do."

"Your own sleep is the path to your nightmares," he replied. "Do you own your nightmares, Mister Shanks, or do they own you?"

"Oh, no, don't you try to spook me! I'm not as gullible as those people who come down here and give you money! Who the hell do you think you are?"

"I thought you understood. This is the river Acheron, and I am Charon, ferryman to the land of the dead."

"Are you, now?" Marcus balked. "And, let's see, so that'd be Hades over there, would it?"

"It would be."

"You know, you don't look Greek."

"I am not."

"Oh, from somewhere else, then? No, don't tell me, I don't want to hear it. I can't decide what's more insane—that you're down here selling that story, or that people are actually buying it. What, someone on the surface hypnotizes people to think they're dead and then sends them through my basement to give you money for a ride?" It struck him as needlessly complicated, but there was probably some reason for it.

"Not all have money. So few know to bring any nowadays, and in truth, I have no use for it. But those who do bring it . . . Surely you've heard that you can't take it with you? So I collect it from them. The clutter left on the shore gets to be quite dreadful otherwise."

"Look, 'Charon,' or whatever, I want to know what you did to those people you took across the river, and I want to know where my girlfriend's cat is."

"I took them across the river. Nothing more."

"But how did you get them to come down here?"

"Everyone crosses the river eventually. I did not 'get' them here. They are dead."

"Right. And did you take Fagles across, too?"

"Fagles?"

"The cat."

"I seem to remember a cat."

"Across the river."

"Yes."

"Fine," Marcus said. "Let's go. I want to cross."

"You cannot."

"Aha!" he shouted. "I can't cross because I haven't been brainwashed yet, can I? Can't have someone thinking rationally see your scam? Pay no attention to the man behind the curtain, eh?"

"You are not dead. It is not your time to see the afterlife."

"Afterlife. Right. Ain't gonna work on me. Religion's just a way to consolidate a power base. This is the twenty-first century. God is dead."

"Yes, that is what Nietzsche said. The look on his face was priceless, let me tell you."

Marcus crossed his arms. "I'm not leaving until you take me."

"I only run the ferry. I don't do the taking. That is Death's job. He hangs about here sometimes, and he gets uptight if I take the living across before he gets to them. Says it messes up the order, and order is his thing, you see. He's a control freak. If you ask me, he has a bit of a stick up his ass, but he does outrank me."

Marcus stood his ground. "I'm not leaving here unless you take me across."

The ferryman huffed and then stared at him as if considering. "You are not going to let it alone, are you?"

Marcus shook his head.

"Then it would seem I have little choice."

"I'm glad we understand each other."

"Oh," the ferryman bent down to pick up the pole. "Do we, now?" His gnarled grip tightened on the pole for a moment before he moved suddenly toward the boat. "Come."

They boarded the boat, and Marcus made sure to sit facing him. The ferryman hefted his weight against the pole and pushed them off from the dock. "I want you to remember," he whispered, "that you requested this. Do not touch the water."

Their progress was slow. The ferryman remained silent so that the only sounds were the lap of the water and the creak of the boat. The silence lengthened the minutes, and the old man's clouded eyes were fixed on Marcus and paid little heed to the piloting of the boat. Unwilling to turn his back, yet feeling a growing unease at meeting the ferryman's gaze, Marcus found himself searching for words to fill the silence.

"Would you stop staring?"

The old man grinned, eyes still fastened to Marcus. "Habit's force, I believe. As I said, I avoid speaking to the dead. They usually turn away if I watch them in silence."

"I'm not turning my back to you," Marcus said.

"You are not dead yet, either."

"Exactly. I'm planning to keep it that way."

"I merely state fact."

Marcus stole a glance at the cliffs that rose against the approaching shore. Still too far. "So how'd you know what Nietzsche said if you don't talk to the dead?"

"Most dead, no. But the philosophers are sometimes interesting. Musicians on occasion."

"Musicians? Seen Elvis?"

"Hasn't everyone?"

"So he is dead, then."

"Oh, quite. But still very nice to his mother, I understand."

"Mm." Marcus rolled his eyes. "What about

Nixon?"

"I tend to row faster with a politician aboard. I may have set a record the day I took him."

What do you know, Marcus thought, a psycho hermit con-man with a sense of humor. "Perhaps you should invest in a motorboat."

"That was tried once."

"And?"

"It upset the dog."

"I didn't see a dog."

"On the other side. Not a," he paused to chuckle, "'mythology' expert, are you?"

"Mythology describes every religion, as far as I'm concerned."

"Tell that to the dog. There is a reason why cats prefer Egypt."

The boat slid ashore with an unceremonious scrape. "The other side," the ferryman announced.

"Do I need to tip you to wait for me now, I suppose?" He climbed out warily. The man made no move against him.

"I have no use for coin, as I said. I will return within the hour." Saying nothing more, he turned the boat back across the black water.

It was dreadfully quiet.

The shoreline there was small—a tiny beach that covered a span of about forty feet between the river and a nearly sheer cliff of sandstone. The only place to go was a single opening in the cliff that led into darkness.

Marcus peered in from the mouth of the tunnel. "Fagles?" His voice echoed and then died.

A faint meow answered.

"Fagles?" he called again and stepped into the tunnel. Only then did he realize that he'd lost his flashlight when he fell in the river. Great.

The meow sounded close. Marcus crept deeper into the blackness, testing each footfall and listening for the cat. Though he went slowly, the blackness soon turned total. Unwilling to touch the wall for fear of finding something unpleasant, he moved straight forward, still calling for Fagles. Each time, the cat answered. It was clearly not happy; the little fur ball was seldom so vocal unless it was disturbed.

He kept going for what felt like fifty yards before the cat's eyes gleamed at him not ten feet ahead. They blinked once and then darted forward to spring at him. Marcus caught the cat on instinct. Thank goodness the little beast was declawed. Unwilling to risk losing him again, he held onto Fagles as best he could and wondered what to do next.

The tunnel was straight. Finding his way back shouldn't be a problem, but he hadn't found out where the "dead" people had gone. Did he want to—

A growl cut through the darkness. The dog! Marcus froze, trying to gauge how far away it was. Fagles began to struggle in his grip.

There was a second growl, louder this time and decidedly hostile. He still could not tell the distance. Marcus slowly took a step backwards. He could come back. Go back to his house, get a flashlight, maybe a baseball bat . . .

A terrible bark shot from up the tunnel, followed by a scramble of claws and limbs. Panicked by the sound in the dark, he dropped Fagles and ran for the tunnel entrance. It was coming, and it was big. He could hear it behind him now, huffing with canine savagery, chasing him. All he could do was run for the beach, find a rock or two, and face the dog in the light. He hated dogs! He bloody hated dogs!

He stumbled, arms flailing in the darkness, and barely managed to regain his balance and find footing on the uneven rock. The beast snarled behind him, closer. Marcus renewed his pace, expecting with every step for the animal to pounce on him from behind.

And then the light of the tunnel loomed, and he was out. He ran to the edge of the shore where Fagles had retreated, scooped up a few large stones, and wheeled to face the dog with an arm raised to throw in his defense.

The scream he heard next was his. The sight alone paralyzed him as his mind clawed at its own sanity trying to reconcile the spectacle standing before him at the mouth of the cave.

It was enormous: the size of a grizzly, but shaped like some horrid wolf. Claws on massive paws scraped the rocks where it stood, its midnight fur bristling, its teeth bared, and its tail—like a giant lizard's—whipping the air behind it. But most terrible were the eyes that stared him down, bloodshot and horrible in their intensity. There were six.

The thing had three heads.

It stopped at the mouth of the cave, watching him with a savage light in those six eyes. Marcus stood rooted to the shore, clutching the rocks he'd scooped and, when fear would let him, struggling to wrap some sort of logical explanation around the creature.

He was still struggling when the old man spoke behind him. "Shall I assume you wish to go back now?"

Marcus didn't take his eyes off the beast. "What the hell is that?!"

"The dog," the ferryman said. "Cerberus! Down, boy!"

Incredibly, the creature stopped snarling and, with a snort, turned and padded contentedly back into the cave.

When he was sure it was gone, Marcus let himself turn to where the ferryman stood in his boat, about ten feet out from the shore. "Those people you brought. . . did it. . . he. . ."

"Did he what?" The old man laughed. "Did he eat them? Of course not, they were dead! He lets them in just fine, he just doesn't let them *out*. But you, as I have said, are not yet dead—something he would gladly rectify if you tried to pass."

No more, Marcus thought. No more insanity! "Okay, you know what? I—I don't think I care anymore what's going on down here—"

"But I have told you."

"—I just want to get back. Now. Take me back!" He didn't want to know what this nightmare was. He just wanted it over. If he could just get back to the house it would all be okay.

The ferryman grinned. "No."

"No? *No?* I have to go! How else do I get back?"

"Oh, there is no other way to get back. You wouldn't survive a swim across these waters. You were lucky enough to wash ashore when you did the first time. And you obviously cannot go forward. I told you, you do not belong. You refused to listen."

"But you can't just leave me trapped here!"

"Can't I? Why should I care if you're trapped? I'm stuck running a ferry at the ass-end of the Underworld for all eternity! You think this is what I wanted to do with my existence? 'It's high-profile!' Hades told me. 'Meet interesting people! Lots of fresh air!' Lying son-of-a-titan. You're only on this river until you starve, then you can go up the tunnel. I'm stuck here until the end of time!"

"Look, fine, whatever! Don't help me! The next time you bring someone over, I'll just take your boat myself!"

"Oh, and can you best me, Marcus?" Charon asked. "Go ahead, hit me with those rocks!"

Anger had Marcus throwing without thinking. The rock shot straight for the ferryman's head and passed right through it. He gaped, and then hurled another, and another. Rock after rock passed through the man until Marcus gave up and collapsed on the ground with a gasp.

"Bit of a problem you have, I would say. There is one other option I can give you: I'll take you back. In exchange, you'll have a week to bask in the glory of returning your girlfriend's pet, but then you're back here to take over this job for me so that I can finally spend some of that money, for six months a year until you die."

Marcus stood up and met the ferryman's gaze. "And if I agree to that," he said, "you'll let me go?"

"If you swear an oath to it, yes."

Marcus regarded the old man. Who said he'd have to keep his word?

*    *    *

The bartender watched the old man pause from his story to drain his glass. "And did he swear?"

The old man grinned. "Well, I am here, aren't

I? Oh, I'm certain he never intended to come back to the river once I took him across, but no one can break an oath made by the river Styx—figuratively or geographically."

"I thought you said it was the Acheron?"

"They're connected," the old man's companion muttered. "It's complicated."

The old man nodded. "At any rate, after his week was up, he woke up there and found he couldn't bear to leave. Another drink, if you please."

"Well, that's one of the more unique stories I've heard told in here," said the bartender as he filled him up. "This one's on me."

"Oh, I've got plenty of money," he said. The old man placed an ingot on the bar. "Here, enjoy it. You never know how long you've got."

The bartender gaped at the gold and then scooped it up with an uneasy thank you before he moved away to the other end of the bar.

The old man's companion watched the bartender go. "Three weeks, five days, seven hours, and . . . seventeen seconds." he whispered.

Charon grunted and took another drink. "Death," he said, "loosen up."

# SNIPE HUNT

The stream burbled in its course beside the forest path as the first few leaves of autumn surfed their way down it. Janette trotted beside the stream, smiling at the water and ignoring the muffled chirping coming from the sack she carried slung over her shoulder.

Snipes really were noisy, but at least this one wasn't struggling too much. She was surprised to have found it at all. Before she'd spotted it sleeping under a tree—with its turtle head, falcon body and raccoon tail just like Jack and Dan had described— she'd suspected that the whole "snipe hunt" idea had just been the latest of her brothers' many attempts to ditch their ten year-old sister. Yet now that she'd caught one, she was glowing with pride. The cold air didn't bother her; the snipe was real! Her brothers finally liked her! And she'd caught it all by herself!

She was skipping and singing, "I caught the snipe!" when she heard the man's laughter.

"Caught a snipe, have you?" She heard his voice before he quite literally appeared on the path before her, wearing a dark riding cloak that matched his thick black hair. "Are you sure about that?" Behind his neat beard the man's smile was friendly, and his English accent made Janette giggle.

"I did!" Janette beamed.

"May I see it?"

She nearly opened the sack, but stopped herself. "Well, it might get out. I don't want it to escape before my brothers see."

The man chuckled. "Things can't escape that haven't been caught. I'm afraid your sack is empty."

The sack suddenly did feel very light. In fact, it felt like nothing at all. She quickly opened it and looked inside. Oh no! "Where is it?" she cried.

"Never there!" he declared with a grin. "Made you see it! The old bait and switch, I do so love that one! My own invention, you know! Played a bit of a trick on you, I'm afraid."

Janette threw the sack to the ground. "That's

not nice!" There was no snipe. Her brothers really had been trying to ditch her. She could feel the tears coming.

"All in good fun!" he said. "Why are you crying?"

She told him.

"Oh, come now, snipe hunts are a tradition! I invented those, too, actually."

"But they're *always* doing it!" she sobbed. "They don't want me around at all!"

The man's smile faded. "Always?"

Janette nodded.

"Well, that does hurt, doesn't it?" He crouched down to her level. "My family's like that, especially my father."

She sniffed. "Your father?"

"Oh, Zeus." He smiled. "You know, king of the gods and all that."

"There's no real Zeus," she said. "You're trying to trick me, too."

"Oh, sure, not anymore. He picked up and left a while ago. 'Hermes,' he said, 'stay behind and look after things.' Took most of the family. Ditching on a pantheonic scale."

Janette recognized the name from the book of Greek myths her dad had given her. Her only friends were books, but they were still just books. "You're not Hermes." She was tired of being tricked.

"Not Hermes? If I weren't Hermes, could I do this?" He suddenly disappeared and then reappeared five feet away, then ten, then twenty. At the last he flew up above her, hung in mid-air, and then slowly floated back to the ground. "God of messengers, scoundrels, and merchants!" he announced with a bow. "Oh, I know what you're thinking: 'Where's the winged sandals? Where's the winged hat?' Truth is, I really don't need them. They're just for show and, quite frankly, hats are rather out of style now."

Janette blinked in amazement. A *real* god? "But . . . why do you have an English accent?"

"Spent a lot of time there in the last thousand years. Zeus always had me carrying messages to Britain to get me off Olympus. When you're the trickster god, people don't always want you around, either. Or maybe it's just because I was the youngest."

"It's no fun being the youngest," Janette said.

"It's hard," he agreed. "Finally, they sent me

out and left when I was gone. But it's not all bad. I did a lot of freelance messenger work after that. You like the King Arthur legend? I did that one! Oh, sure, the Muses want credit for getting it written, but who do you think handled the distribution? It was the middle of the twelfth century. Moveable type printing wasn't even around until 1455! I met Shakespeare later, too."

"I'm only ten. I don't know much about him."

"Oh, he was the bomb, as you kids say. I learned *that* phrase on the Internet." His face soured. "Great thing, the Internet: global, instant communication everywhere. Of course, I might like it more if it hadn't cost me my *bloody job!*" He suddenly flashed a dazzling, perfect smile. "Not that I'm bitter, of course."

"You didn't invent that, too?" Janette asked. He did seem to take credit for a lot.

"The Internet? Of course not. That was Al Gore, the bugger. Not much for me to do now but play jokes on people. Not that that isn't fun."

"It's not fun if people are always playing jokes on *you*."

"No, rather not, I'd say," Hermes answered. "Maybe you ought to turn the tables."

Janette looked up at the god and smiled.

*  *  *

Fifteen minutes later, Janette stepped from the bushes where Jack and Dan were playing on the riverbank and throwing stones at the birds.

"Find a snipe yet, Janette?" Jack asked with a grin at his brother.

"Uh huh!" she said happily.

Dan snorted. "Oh, yeah? Then where is it?"

"Behind me."

At that, the bushes shook violently and a giant beast forced its way through them to tower over Jack and Dan. Its great turtle's head opened its mouth to brandish jagged fangs and shake the sky with a thunderous roar. Immense wings buffeted the air as it stepped toward her brothers with an angry swish of its great striped tail.

"It wouldn't fit in the sack," Janette said innocently.

When Jack and Dan had torn off screaming into the woods, the giant snipe shifted and became Hermes again. Janette shook with uncontrollable giggling. "That was too cool!" she squealed.

"Told you it'd be fun," Hermes said.

She giggled. "They're gonna be mad at me."

"Oh, but they had it coming, didn't they?" He grinned at her. "I'm just sorry we couldn't include a giant wooden horse somehow. I still can't believe they fell for that one!"

# PLAYING WITH HUBRIS

The night the "god" first spoke to me, the café was crowded. At nine p.m. on a weekday, it was rare that it would be anything but. I stood at the top of the stairway landing searching for a seat. The café, situated on the mezzanine level of a large bookstore, was my usual writing haunt. Its proximity to a university campus ensured that it would be filled with college students seeking distraction from the books they had spread out across the tables where they sat. I had graduated four years ago myself, but it still felt like the perfect place to write.

If I could find a table.

But the seating gods did smile upon me that evening, and I slipped into a table by the edge of the balcony as two women packed up their things. A friendly smile and a tall mocha later, I was comfortably situated, pen in hand, staring at a blank page. It was the same blank page I'd stared at the previous night. And the night before that. Nothing was coming to me. I twirled my pen and looked across the faces in the café, seeing nothing. I closed my eyes and searched the back of my eyelids for inspiration that wasn't there. I looked back down at the page and willed the words to come.

Nothing.

"I beg your pardon, but might I make use of this chair?" I looked up at the man who had spoken. He was tall, comfortably dressed in a formal Eddie Bauer sort of way, and had his hand resting on the top of the empty chair across the table from me.

"Hmm? Oh, go ahead," I told him. Suddenly conscious of the conspicuously blank page before me, I pulled open my writing folder and made a show of leafing through it to appear busy while I waited for him to take the chair away.

The man left it where it was and sat down at my table instead.

"Ah . . . oh," I said in surprise. "I'm sorry, I didn't know that's what you meant." I pulled my paper and mocha a little closer to give him some room on the small surface.

"You don't mind, I hope? It's just myself and my tea. I abhor standing and drinking, and there are no open tables."

"Oh, no, that's fine," I said, attempting to be amicable. In truth, I did mind a little. It's harder for me to write if I feel someone is watching me. But I wasn't the sort to deny a seat if asked.

"You mind a little, I think," the stranger said with a smile, "but I thank you for your sacrifice."

I wasn't quite sure what to say to that. He sounded sincere enough. I just nodded and went back to my blank page.

The man took a sip from his cup. "How's the writing coming?" he asked.

I chuckled uncomfortably and motioned to the white space. "See for yourself."

"I mean in general," he said. "Heard anything back from the agents you queried?"

I put my pen down and looked at him. "Do I know you?" I saw nothing readily familiar in his face. His features were strong, but not recognizable.

"Oh, not personally, no," he smiled. There was something of a twinkle in the experienced depths of his eyes. "I should certainly think you know *of* me, however." He offered his hand. "Phoebus Apollo." I was shaking his hand before I could reply. His grip was powerful but measured. "Don't mind the Phoebus, though. So few people use it anymore."

I withdrew my hand. "You're saying you're Apollo. The god."

He smiled disarmingly. "Well, not 'god' in the sense that people use the word these days, but yes."

I gave him a couple more cynical blinks. He certainly seemed a well-dressed psychotic. "God of music, of medicine . . . drives the sun across the sky and all that?"

"None other than," he agreed. "Though I don't actually drive the sun anymore. They've got that whole thing all automated now. Upkeep on the chariot got to be too much of an expense. Progress, you know."

"Right."

"You don't believe me," he said, unsurprised.

"Does that bother you?"

He laughed once and waved his hand in dismissal. "Oh, certainly not. I've had temples built in my honor. I don't need *your* approval."

"Oh? I thought you guys were supposed to be all ego. And shouldn't you be appearing in the form of a bull or something?"

"Hey, don't be confusing me with my dad. That whole 'carry off the maiden in bull form' was his favorite pastime." He rolled his eyes. "*Every* Wednesday night."

"It's a wonder Hera put up with him," I said, humoring him. I took a few Classics courses in college, myself.

"Well, when you're the goddess that people come to for blessing their marriages, you have to put up with a lot. And being married to the king of the whole pantheon is likely worth something to her."

"She must have a lot of issues."

"She's just my stepmother, so we hardly talk much. I believe you Americans would call it a dysfunctional family. Last I heard, she'd been elected to the Senate."

"Ah," I said. He settled into his chair and just smiled at me. If there were a god of awkward moments, he'd have been at the table, too. "Well, I'd better be going." I stood up so quickly as I gathered my things together that I had to make a grab for my pen before it fell to the floor.

"You didn't answer my question," he said.

"Question?" I replied and shoved my folder

into my bag. "Oh, sorry about that. I really need to run. Table's all yours." Pulling my coat off the back of the chair, I strode out quickly before he could say any more.

\* \* \*

The café was even more crowded the following night. I was standing on the top of the landing, waiting for a table to clear when his voice spoke up beside me. "You're really playing with hubris, you know."

I struggled to keep from groaning and turned to face him. He had snuck up when I wasn't looking and was now leaning on the railing beside me in a formal tuxedo. "Hubris, eh?" I asked, adding, "Nice tux."

"Walking out on a god when he comes to visit. Just a trifle prideful, wouldn't you say? I have to be a little more patient nowadays, but even a god's patience has limits. Three thousand years ago you'd have gotten an arrow in your rump. And yes, it is a nice tux."

I continued my watch of the tables. "Yeah, well, I guess godhood isn't all that it used to be, huh?"

"You're telling me. Some of us aren't even in the business anymore. Christianity really knocked the bottom out of the market. Now *there's* a monopoly. Hermes doesn't even bother nowadays. Didn't see the point once the Internet got going. Hestia got out a long time ago. And Hephaestus, mighty god of the forge? He says they don't need him anymore with all the assembly lines." He suddenly grinned and elbowed me. "Then again, you get married to the goddess of love and you suddenly want to stay home a lot more, eh?"

"Aphrodite?" I asked. "Did she hang it up, too?" I couldn't resist being just a little amused at the concept.

"What, are you kidding?" he answered. "She also deals in lust and beauty, you know. Almost your entire entertainment industry is a living temple to her—if you don't count PBS. Only Hades and Ares are doing so well. Oh, she's still at it, make no mistake."

"Mm," I grunted.

"You've still not answered this god's question from last night."

"Which was that again?"

He scowled. "People used to come from miles and miles to my temple at Delphi to hear my words. They would not forget them so easily."

I'd had enough. "Look, if you're really a god,

prove it. Can't you wave your hand and get us an open table?"

"You are being exceedingly demanding for a mortal," he replied. "And, alas, such a thing is beyond even me. The availability of open café tables is the purview of the Fates alone, whom not even Zeus will challenge."

I had to laugh at that. "Good answer. Convenient, too."

"I only speak the truth."

"So no table."

"I'll agree to tell you how soon one will open up if you answer my questions from last night."

"My memory's not that good. You'll have to repeat them."

He sighed. "How is your writing coming, and have you heard back from any of the four agents you queried in the past month?"

Okay, that was weird. "If I tell you, will you tell me how you knew I'd queried four?"

"Alright," he agreed. "But I can't promise you'll like the answer."

Oh, goodie. I didn't see a point in arguing about it. "I've finished my first novel and I'm working on the second. But lately, I'm trying to get some short stories published to better attract an agent. Unfortunately, the blank page you saw me staring at last night is the sum total of the story ideas I've come up with to date. As for my agent queries, two said I wasn't what they're looking for, and the other two haven't gotten back to me, yet." I paused to take a breath. "Now how did you know it was four?"

"I'm Apollo," he said with a perfect smile. I didn't bother to hide my scowl from him. "I said you wouldn't like the answer."

I scanned the café again for a seat. If I didn't see one soon, I was leaving. "I thought you guys weren't omniscient?"

"We're not, but that doesn't mean we don't pay attention to things. I've been watching you."

"So you're stalking me."

"Well that's hardly complimentary. I *was* going to offer you my help."

I tried not to be rude. "No, thank you. I'm fine."

"What about your blank sheet of paper?"

My writer's insecurity flared in me and the defenses went up. "I don't want any help!" I whispered. "I especially don't want the help of some nut with a god-complex!"

He suddenly seemed to grow taller, and for a moment his eyes flared, burning down at me. I had just enough time to curse myself for attacking the delusions of a madman before the glare evaporated a moment later.

"Things were so much simpler three thousand years ago," he said almost wistfully. "There's an open table."

I blinked in surprise a moment before following his shifted gaze to a table along the wall whose occupant was packing his things.

"Thank you," I said with finality and started forward. "I'd prefer to sit alone, if you don't mind." It was more assertive than I usually was, but after what I'd already said to the man, it didn't seem like that mattered. Without waiting for a response, I moved towards the table.

After crossing through two study groups, I arrived at my desired table as the current occupant stood up to leave. I nodded a greeting to him as he gathered up his jacket and then glanced back behind me to make sure my deity friend hadn't tried to join me. To my relief, he had apparently left altogether.

The young woman I bumped into when I

turned back to sit down had the reddest hair I'd ever seen.

"Oh, geez," I stammered. "Sorry, I didn't know you were— I mean I didn't see you and then I turned around and—" I stopped, feeling like a bit of an idiot.

She laughed in an almost lyrical fashion. "Looks like you're trying to steal my table," she joked with a smile.

"Your—? Ah," I managed.

"I was over there waiting for it," she continued pleasantly, indicating the café counter. "But I don't need much room. Want to share?"

I sighed with a bit of relief. "Thank you," I told her. Sharing a table with a delusional, middle-aged man was one thing. Sharing it with an attractive woman was quite another. Was that a form of sexism? I watched a moment as she set a Douglas Adams book on the table and then turned to fish in her bag in a way that brushed the ends of that fiery hair across her neck and shoulders. Perhaps not sexist as much as socially selective. I decided I should probably say something before she got too engrossed in her reading.

"It's crowded tonight," I tried. "I just spent about ten minutes on the landing talking to a guy who thinks he's a god."

"Yes, I saw you waiting there," she laughed as she pulled out a pair of glasses. "Which one?"

I looked around. "Oh, I think he left," I told her. "He was the one in the tux. Kind of hard to miss in here."

She chuckled. She seemed to do that a lot, though not in an off-putting sort of way. Maybe she was just nervous. Something gave me the impression that she was more than just amazing hair and a laugh. Perhaps it was a side effect of the glasses.

"No." She smiled. "I mean, which god?"

"Oh." My turn to chuckle. "Apollo."

"Apollo," she repeated, sounding impressed. "Helpful guy to have around."

"Oh, if he were the real thing, sure. I'm trying to get a book published. I could use a little divine intervention. I'm Greg, by the way." I added.

"Thalia," she returned. "So you need help with your writing?"

"I could certainly use some inspiration, yes. I'm trying to work on some short stories, but after concentrating on a novel for so long, it's hard to shift gears."

"And those silly agents won't even give you a second look if you're not published somewhere." She smiled compassionately.

"There's a little hope. I'm still waiting to hear back from two of them, but . . ." I trailed off.

"You're afraid they'd say the same thing as the last two?" I nodded and was about to go on complaining when something occurred to me. "How'd you know about the last two?"

She giggled uncomfortably. "Well, you said you'd had trouble getting an agent, so I assumed you'd already sent to some . . ."

"Actually, I didn't. You brought the agents up."

"Really? I could have sworn—"

"And you knew I'd sent to four this month."

"No, really," she stammered. "I . . . oh, zut! I'm just not good at this whole subterfuge thing!"

I sighed. "The man in the tux sent you, didn't he?"

She pouted. "Oh, if I come out and tell you, he'll be upset with me. It's just not fair! I'm not a spy, that's not what I do. I think it's terribly unfair of him to ask me to do this without telling you, don't you? I mean, honestly, it's positively unheard of!"

"Do you want to let me in on just what's going on here?" I asked. I was trying to put as much irritation as I could into my voice, but watching this woman pout right in front of me was keeping me from doing it well.

"Oh, this would be so much easier if you'd just start writing, you know. Why don't you try that right now? Maybe you'll get an idea?"

There was something of an urge to write in me then, but that urge was overshadowed by a surge of irritation over what business it was of either of these two. "Who are you?"

"I'm Thalia!" she cried, as if that explained everything. I continued waiting for more until she rolled her eyes and continued, "Thalia! The *muse*?"

"Oh!" I declared. "Thalia the *muse*! Well why didn't I think of that? I met Apollo, now I'm talking to a muse! I suppose that dog on a leash outside the store is Cerberus? I mean, he's missing two heads, but what do I know, right?"

"Apollo said you wouldn't believe me if I told you. And now I've blown it and you don't believe in me, either and . . ." Her eyes softened as if she were suddenly on the verge of tears. "And now it's just ruined, it's all ruined!"

The look on her face tugged at my sympathy and I couldn't help wanting to calm her down somehow. "Alright, alright. It's okay. Which one are you?"

"What?" she said, dabbing her eyes with a napkin.

"Well, it's been a while since I took a class on this, but don't the nine muses each cover a different sort of writing?"

She nodded. "Comedy and science fiction," she said with a little smile.

I blinked. I was doing that quite a lot lately. "Comedy and . . . science fiction? I wasn't aware the ancient Greeks did sci-fi."

Her face continued to brighten slightly. "Well, of course they didn't, silly. But when the modern genres started popping up, we muses had to take on more responsibilities."

"Uh, huh. And how's that going for you?"

"Oh, it takes some getting used to. For centuries I was a specialist. Doing both at once took a bit of juggling. But I've . . . mostly got it down now." She paused a moment and blushed.

"Mostly?"

"Well . . ." She was giggling nervously again.

"Sometimes . . . just every once in a while, understand, sometimes I forget which I'm doing—just for a minute, you see—but then it's too late and they both run together."

"I don't follow."

"I mean, it's like making lasagna and chocolate cake in the same pan. Separately, they're great, but mixed together, neither of them come out right." Her voice started to shake and she began to tear up again. "But it was just a little slip up," she said. "It's not *my* fault it was the prequel to the most successful sci-fi trilogy in the history of cinema! It was just one character! How much can one character do!"

"Are you saying . . .?"

"I gave him the inspiration for Jar-Jar!" she blurted.

My eyes widened. "That's *your* fault?"

She burst into tears. "Don't say it like that!" she sobbed. "I just made the suggestion! George is the one who wrote it down!" Her voice was rising higher and louder, word by word, until she finally shrieked out, "And—and now everybody *hates* me!"

An entire café's worth of heads turned our way

as I sat and tried to figure out what to say to this hysterically delusional woman. Before I could think of if or how I should comfort her, she grabbed her things and stood up in such a rush that she nearly knocked the table over. "I can't do this!" she burst, choking back tears. "I don't care what he says. You've got me upset and I can't create when I'm upset. Maybe Melpomene can, but . . . I just have to go!"

She dashed out as I stood up, leaving me to watch her blazing hair bounce down the stairs and wonder just what in the name of Hades had happened.

\* \* \*

I didn't go back to the café the next night. I told myself I'd had a long day at work and I just didn't have the energy, but to be honest, I was so afraid of running into one of them—either of them, "god" or "muse"—that I almost stayed home the following night, too. But my pride finally got the better of me. That was *my* café, and I wasn't going to let two bad nights keep me away.

Nine o'clock found me bounding up the stairs and passing three women going down who thankfully did not claim to be The Fates. (They weren't even carrying scissors.)

I found a seat right off and, as money was a little tight, sat down with just an oatmeal cookie and a glass of water. That night I wasn't feeling like writing and instead leafed through a writer's magazine looking at contests.

"Wouldn't you need to get over your writer's block before you enter any contests?" I knew who it was. I didn't even look up at him.

"I'm looking for inspiration," I said. "Go away."

"A contest inspired the Trojan War," he continued. "Dreadful business."

"Yeah, I know all about it," I said, turning a page in the magazine. "I read The Iliad, too."

Golden light suddenly blazed forth from where the man stood. Every sound in the café ceased. Every movement stopped.

"I was there." His voice was thick with power.

He sat down at the table with me. The tux of the previous night had been replaced with an Armani suit. His eyes settled on me with a weight I could feel. It wasn't an oppressive weight, but more like the sense you feel when standing in a great stone cathedral or temple. Age, history, and the massiveness of the architecture—all of those same feelings fell upon me in that simple café.

"It's much better in the original Greek," he added in a voice that had softened slightly from a moment before. "Though I don't suppose you've studied Greek."

My mouth opened. At least I think it did. At the time, my brain was too occupied with trying to get a handle on the situation to come up with something to say. Everything had stopped. Cups of unmoving liquid were held poised before anticipating mouths. Faces were frozen in mid-sentence. The silence was complete but for his voice and my own breathing (I only just then had remembered to tell myself to breathe). Either the cookie had an extra-special ingredient, or I was actually sitting with a god.

"Uh . . ." I managed.

"Impressive trick, isn't it?" Apollo asked. "Take my advice. Don't bother trying to comprehend it. It's not worth thinking about."

"How . . .?"

"I'm a god. I told you not to bother thinking about it." While I kept thinking about it, he paused a moment before continuing. "If you'd only been this silent the other night when you met Thalia. Do you know it took her a full day just to stop crying?

That whole movie is a very sensitive subject for her. She's better now, of course, but don't bring it up again."

I suddenly stopped gaping and defended myself. "Well, she's the one that brought it up!" I shot. "And why didn't you do this before?"

The god's eyebrows arched. "Do which? Stop time?"

"Uh, *yeah*!" I said with a glare until I thought better of it. "Well, I mean— I didn't mean to yell at you there, but. . ."

"Ah, so it seems you're learning a little respect at last!"

"Um, well, you know what they say: Never yell at live dragons. Or something like that."

"Dragons? My dear mortal, there are no dragons!" he chuckled. "Though I suppose your imagination deserves applauding."

There came from behind me a giggle and a familiar voice. "Definition of irony: a god telling a mortal there are no dragons."

"Oh, come now, Thalia," Apollo told her, "that would imply that we gods don't exist."

Thalia walked up to us holding a bottle of cranberry juice. Her red hair blazed over shoulders left bare by a simple black dress. "That's what he thought a few minutes ago."

"So . . . you're really interested in my writing?" I asked.

"Oh, yes," said the god. "We who live on the peaks of many-ridged Olympus all have our responsibilities. We're all gods *of* something, you see. If we don't keep our houses in order, we fade. I'm the god of music and poetry, among other things. Do I have to paint you a picture?"

Thalia pulled a chair out for herself and sat. "He tried to help you before, but you wouldn't have him. Then he sent me to attempt to inspire you, but we all know how that turned out."

"I didn't take you seriously! If you'd just done this in the first place . . ." I waved my hands at the frozen patrons.

Apollo looked at the muse. I did too. (Hey, she was nice to look at.) "He doesn't get it."

"George was like this too," she said with a frown. She turned to me. "You're a writer. You conjure people and worlds out of thin air. You can create so much and all you need is the imagination to do it."

"It was a test," I said, beginning to understand.

"It wasn't a test," corrected the god. (Okay, so maybe I wasn't understanding.) "It was more of an exercise. To see if you could open your mind to the possibilities of believing a Greek god and a muse were visiting you in a café. Did you ever stop to think 'What if?' 'What if that man is telling the truth?' 'What if he really is the god he says he is?' 'What if all of the beings you read about in myths truly existed?' If you're not allowing yourself to be open to possibilities, it's no wonder you're dry of ideas."

I nodded. I hadn't, really. I hadn't even been thinking of questions like that when I was trying to come up with a story. "I still feel like I failed a test."

"Perhaps," Apollo agreed. "But victories seldom teach as much as defeats."

"And there's certainly still hope for you," Thalia assured me. "What better way to broaden your imagination than to have something like this happen?"

I don't recall exactly what I had planned to say in response to that. I never got to say it. Immediately after, the god waved his hand, and the entire café exploded into motion once more. The crash of a dish hitting the floor jerked my attention behind me for just a moment. When I turned back to the table, Apollo and Thalia had vanished.

It's now eleven o'clock at night. They're closing the café and kicking me out. My hand is cramped from writing so much. A few days ago I met a god. Tonight he told me dragons don't exist. Tomorrow night I'm going to use the rest of the blank pages I have to prove him wrong.

## AN EXCERPT FROM THE NOVEL ZEUS IS DEAD: A MONSTROUSLY INCONVENIENT ADVENTURE

Apollo made his way to his own quarters, located in the eastern wing overlooking the secondary stables. (Not a day went by that he wasn't thankful for the olfactory shield Hestia had invented to contain the smell. Apollo loved the fire-breathing horses that once guided the sun chariots, but they subsisted on a steady diet of sulfur and chili.) His footsteps echoed on the polished marble floor. He was out of time for the moment. Work awaited him, again. Dreading the number of messages surely stalking his inbox, he climbed the stairs past the Muses' quarters on the way to his office.

"Are they *insane?*" The question burst from the Muses' quarters, leaving no doubt about the opinion of the one posing it. "How is that the same?

No, answer me! How is that the same!"

Apollo halted his climb and turned instead toward the doorway to poke his head through the silk divider curtains. Thalia stalked back and forth in the middle of the atrium, red hair blazing behind her in the sunlight. She focused all her attention on the phone clutched in her hand.

"No, look!" Thalia caught sight of Apollo and put him off with a nod before directing her ire back into the phone. "I don't care how much of an advance he's getting. You tell those producers the character stays as is or you're backing out! . . . Who *cares* if there's a contract? This is—I'm a Muse! I inspired that whole story! I—" She squeezed her eyes shut to trap welling tears and turned her back. "Fine!" she managed. "Just—fine! You just tell Mr. Brown he'll—he'll have to write the next book without me!" She jammed a finger at the screen to end the call and took a few steps toward the window, her breath ragged, her back to Apollo.

"Thalia?" he tried. "Are—?"

She cut him off with a scream culminating in her hurling the phone against a nearby couch. It barely bounced, landing on the cushion in still-pristine condition. She turned on him.

"If you take the character of a jaded, balding,

wheelchair-bound mathematician in his late fifties and turn him into a female twenty-two- year-old blonde ex-gymnast stripper who's just 'good with numbers,' how does that possibly retain the spirit of the story? Why can't so-called 'creative' executives leave well enough alone? Or hurl themselves off a cliff? Can I shove one off a cliff, Apollo? It would make me ever so happy." She smiled with one of her better doe-eyed expressions.

He smiled back, despite his troubles. "Probably not the best idea, Thalia."

She heaved a sigh and picked up her phone again to polish it. "It wouldn't have to be a big cliff." Eyelashes fluttered at him.

"Stressed?"

She wiped the remnants of a tear. "No? Me? Stressed? No, not at all. Why do you ask?"

"I—"

She hurled herself backward onto the couch. "It's not that every single mortal seems to be invoking us for inspiration for their work. It's really not. I mean it's positively risible that every single slack-jaw on the Internet begs for comedic inspiration each time they make a smart-assed crack on a forum; I can more or less keep my sanity by just ignoring them. But dear gods, it's having to sift through it all!"

"Reminds me of—"

"But hey, I'm a big girl. I can do that, right?" She thrust her fingers into her hair and mussed it, her coiffure looking like a poofed dandelion as she cut him off. "I mean sanity's overrated anyway, isn't it? Got to find the really deserving writers and such out there amid the offal, don't we? Very well, so I'll miss a few gems in the sifting, but hey, them's the breaks, that's luck, not meant to be, right?"

Thalia suddenly caught her reflection in the mirror that made up half of one wall, and her tirade of annoyance continued unabated with a, "Sakes alive, look at my hair!" In a single sweep of her hand, it was perfectly coifed again. Thalia launched a wide-eyed grin at him that all but screamed, "Ta-da!"

Apollo tried to stay on topic. "I suppose that given—"

"But it's—ugh! It's those executives!" She jumped to her feet again. "Those studios and producers and focus groups and—and just the diabolical dumbing-down that everyone seems to think is compulsory! It's driving me positively ape-shit! I mean, excuse me, I know that's not very becoming, but oh my gods, Apollo!" She unscrewed a bottle of ambrosia and began to pour out a glass without offering any to him. "You just shouldn't take a 1,000-page novel and turn it into a two-hour movie! It doesn't work! Do you know how many scripts I've inspired since we came back? I mean just scripts, not even books being made into scripts! Every single one of them altered by philistines who think they know better than a Muse! More breasts! More explosions! More fart jokes! *Fart jokes!* Jiggle-boom-fart-bounce-fart! It's the nimrod anthem!" She suddenly stopped, considering. "Nimrod." She giggled. "I like that word."

As Thalia took the opportunity to down the ambrosia, Apollo took the opportunity to get out a full sentence or two. "You've inspired scripts that were changed before. Before we came back into public awareness. It didn't seem to bother you so much then."

Thalia finished the glass and poured another. "Yes, but it's happening more now. Cumulating, drop by drop!" She sighed again, looking at the full glass before setting it down. "Anyway, I'm being boorish, aren't I? Hi there. How're you?" She forced a dazzling smile and flashed her lashes again.

He laughed. "Trust me; you don't want to know."

"Oh hmm, that certainly doesn't make me curious at all."

"I've been a bit out of touch. Do you know if your sisters are having the same cliff-shoving urges?"

She shrugged. "More or less. I mean except Urania. You know, I still don't see why I got science fiction and she didn't."

Years ago, as the modern genres came into being, the Muses each took on new duties. Thalia added sci-fi to her existing purviews of comedy and poems about farming.

"You picked it yourself. You like science fiction."

"Oh there you go, bringing facts into the argument. She muses astronomy; you should've made her take it. She's got, like, zero workload."

"You drew lots. She picked last. It's your own fault."

"She's only got to worry about astronomy texts, calendar photos, and those stupid little sayings on coffee cups!"

"And bathroom wall graffiti."

Thalia snorted and then blushed at the sound. "Oh, yeah. Maybe she's been talking to those executives."

Apollo walked to the window and gazed out over the stables. Thalia, perhaps sensing he was weighting some sort of decision, said nothing. Her uncharacteristic silence was actually more distracting.

"Thalia," he said at last, "gather your sisters. There's something we must speak about. Don't tell anyone else."

"Ooh, secretive. Sounds like fun. Give me a couple of hours to get them all here."

Apollo shook his head. "Not here. Not on Olympus."

Thalia nodded, perplexed. "Would this have anything to do with cliffs?" she asked. "I've got one all picked out."

### 

**Read more in *Zeus Is Dead: A Monstrously Inconvenient Adventure*, the award-winning comedic fantasy set in a version of our world where reality TV heroes slay actual monsters and the Greek gods have their own Twitter feeds...**

Thanks for reading! If you enjoyed *Mythed Connections*, please consider leaving a review online.

Don't forget to grab *Zeus Is Dead: A Monstrously Inconvenient Adventure*, the award-winning comedic fantasy novel that grew out of the stories you just enjoyed.

And while we're on the subject of things not to forget, don't forget to breathe and maybe eat something now and then, I guess.

# ABOUT THE AUTHOR

An award-winning writer of speculative fiction, Michael G. Munz was born in Pennsylvania but moved to Washington State in 1977 at the age of three. Unable to escape the state's gravity, he has spent most of his life there and studied writing at the University of Washington.

Michael developed his creative bug in college, writing and filming four exceedingly amateur films before setting his sights on becoming a novelist. Driving this goal is the desire to tell entertaining stories that give to others the same pleasure as other writers have given to him. He enjoys writing tales that combine the modern world with the futuristic or fantastic.

Michael has traveled to three continents, and has an interest in Celtic and Greco-Roman mythology. He resides in Seattle where he continues his quest to write the most entertaining novel known to humankind and find a really fantastic clam linguini.

**Connect with Michael online:**
Website: www.michaelgmunz.com
Twitter: @TheWriteMunz
Facebook: www.facebook.com/MichaelGMunz

*(This space intentionally left blank.)*

*(This space unintentionally left blank. Not really sure how that happened.)*

.

*(This space: the final frontier. These are the voyages of the Starship Blank.)*

.

*(Okay, you can stop turning pages now.)*

.

Made in the USA
Middletown, DE
03 February 2021